LEE

N GRAY

By N Gray

Shifter Days, Vampire Nights & Demons in Between

Twisted

Lady Hawk and Her Mountain Man

Hidden Shifter

Wolf

Wolf Retreat

Night Hunter

The Fixer

Kai

Lee

Flynn

Jude

Scout Thorne

The Secret Tomb

Murder of Crows

Blaire Thorne

Ulysses Exposed

Voodoo Priest

Butterflies and Hurricanes

Salvation

Underworld Legacy

The Dana Mulder Suspense Thriller Series

Deadly Pattern

Devil Mountain

Chasing Evil

Nightcrawler

Horror

What's for Dinner

Creature Features

Monster Features

Thrillers

Lady Killer

More from N Gray

writing as Natalie Michaels

Steve Campbell Psychological Suspense Thrillers

The Last Girl

The Bone Forest

The White Dahlia

I See You

Death in the City

More from N Gray

writing as SD Syns

The Diaries

Red Lace Diaries

www.ngraybooks.com

Vinci Books

vinci-books.com

Published by Vinci Books Ltd in 2026

1

Copyright © N Gray 2023

The author has asserted their moral right to be identified as the author of this work in accordance with the Copyright, Designs and Patents Act 1988. This work is a work of fiction. Names, characters, places and incidents are the product of the author's imagination or are used fictitiously. Any resemblance to actual persons, living or dead, places and incidents is entirely coincidental.
All rights reserved. No part of this publication may be copied, reproduced, distributed, stored in any retrieval system, or transmitted in any form or by any means, including photocopying, recording, or other electronic or mechanical methods, nor used as a source for any form of machine learning including AI datasets, without the prior written permission of the publisher.
The publisher and the author have made every effort to obtain permissions for any third party material used in this book and to comply with copyright law. Any queries in this respect should be brought to the attention of the publisher and any omissions will be corrected in future editions.
A CIP catalogue record for this book is available from the British Library.
Paperback ISBN: 9781036702250
The EU GPSR authorised representative is Logos Europe, 9 rue Nicolas Poussion, 17000 La Rochelle, France contact@logoseurope.eu

Chapter One

I narrowed my eyes at Kai. He draped his arm lovingly around Naomi's shoulders, pulling her closer, and kissed her temple. I groaned inwardly at their public display of affection or my lack thereof. If they weren't such a cute couple, I would've slapped Kai just for the fun of it.

"Sorry, brother, I know it's your birthday, but Naomi and I are going away for the weekend," Kai said, wiggling his eyebrows.

"But why Camping? Of all the various activities, you go and decide to camp." I grumbled, not impressed. "You have a forest as a backyard," — the forest was near the warehouse, — "we hunt in the forest when the moon is full and now you want to camp in a forest…" I felt the lines between my eyes deepen.

When Kai kissed Naomi instead of responding, I continued speaking, "Where are you going and can I come with?" I grinned when Kai abruptly stopped showering his wife with love to show how disgusted he was with my comment.

"No, dude, it's our anniversary weekend away," Kai said, pushing against my shoulder. "And we aren't into threesomes." He held Naomi tighter as she giggled at our bantering. "But thanks for the offer anyway. If I'm ever desperate enough to make extra cash, I'll pimp your ass out to the bears. I hear they prefer smaller guys."

I couldn't help but laugh and admire my friend; he was one of a kind. "Good luck getting money out of anyone. Besides, you know I'll do it for free," I said, wiggling my eyebrows. We laughed at my terrible response.

Once I sobered, I added, "I get it, I really do. Enjoy your weekend lovebirds." I brought Naomi in for a hug and fist bumped Kai at the same time. "How long are you going away for? And does the boss know?" I glanced over my shoulder at the warehouse we called home.

"Yeah, I told Léon. He says it's fine." He slapped Naomi's ass when she walked away, sashaying. "I gotta go, brother," he said, grinning and wiggling his eyebrows.

"Don't worry," Flynn said, draping his arm around my shoulders. I narrowed my eyes at the were-lion; I should've heard him sneak up on me yet somehow I didn't. "I'll look after this one," Flynn added. "We all know he can't function like a man without his bestie."

I punched him in his stomach.

"Oof, easy there, leopard," he said, feigning injury.

"Back off, lion," I growled, pushing him away from me.

Flynn grinned, knowing he had succeeded in irritating me. It was one thing working with other shifters, but a different situation living with them, too.

Kai and I shared the same security shifts at the warehouse with two other shifters; Flynn, a were-lion, and Jude, a were-tiger. The four of us got on just fine but every now and then, like today, either Flynn or Jude irritated the crap out of me.

Léon, the Master Vampire of Sterling Meadow, had been around for centuries and had collected many items, some of which no one had been privy to seeing other than him. His priceless artifacts were kept at the warehouse we guarded because no insurance company could afford to insure the contents.

"Are we going out tonight?" Flynn asked enthusiastically.

I exhaled audibly and stared at him suspiciously. "Yeah, I suppose so. Why?"

"Okay, boys, I must go," Kai said, interrupting us. "See you in a couple of days." He waved over his shoulder as he walked toward his wife, who waited patiently for him at their vehicle, wearing a loving smile that would make any man's heart burst with pride.

"Don't you just hate those love-birds," Flynn added, heading back toward the warehouse. "Anyway, I'm going to check in with Jude and make sure he isn't breaking anything, then we can head out. I'm in desperate need of some tender flesh against my rock hard body."

"Me, too," I whispered.

"I hear you, buddy," Flynn called over his shoulder. "We're still waiting for our happily ever after." He stopped walking, turned around and glanced at me over his sunglasses, his yellow eyes blazing.

I tipped my head slightly in recognition. We were hard asses with our tough exterior, and like most shifters we needed to keep up with a certain facade, but deep down we all wanted to find our special someone. We all wanted the half of what we were missing to make us whole again.

Kai had just about given up when he met Naomi in the

club and they hit it off immediately, although they ran into some trouble with her father. But Kai had found his mate, and he couldn't be happier.

I sighed.

I needed to get my head out of the clouds and focus on securing the warehouse before heading out for drinks.

Chapter Two

It was my birthday, and I stood alone outside the bar like an idiot. Flynn had to rush back to the warehouse to help Jude with a huge delivery nobody warned us about. My usual wingman, Kai, was on a weekend away with his babe and I had… no-one.

I grunted my dissatisfaction regarding my predicament, glanced left and right, and groaned as groups of people headed my way. They laughed, some were drunk and tripped over their feet, while others spoke in hushed tones. They were human and just a group of friends enjoying their evening.

A jealously I hadn't felt in a long time struck with vengeance. Watching the group of friends made me realize how much I wanted a normal life filled with laughter and jealousy and evenings where I'd get drunk and sleep with an amazing woman who only wanted me more than any other man in the world.

But I knew I couldn't have any of that; my life was different. I was different. Everything about my job was different. I had to drink bottles of alcohol by myself before I felt the buzz and sleeping with a human female might hurt her if I wasn't careful. Everything I did had to be carefully thought about before I dared doing it.

I was stronger than most shifters and could kill a human male easily. Everything about my life as a supernatural in a human world was just that... different.

The group of laughing humans approached and the jealousy within me grew. Not wanting it to consume me, I had to get away from the humans and peered at the bar door, growling frustratingly. I didn't want to go back to the warehouse to stare at the television screen and I was tired of doing the same things daily. I needed a break and a change in scenery.

Instead of feeling sorry for myself I entered the local bar, warm air hitting me in the face before I had a chance to exhale. I hung my coat on the last empty hook near the door and scanned the venue for an open seat.

I headed toward the only available seat in a corner at the bar and, as I was about to sit, a curvy pint-sized woman stole the seat and called the barman to order a drink.

I growled.

Under normal circumstances I wouldn't behave aggressively toward a woman but she stole my seat on purpose. She knew I was about to sit down when she slid up beside me and took my seat. And the fact that she didn't bat an eyelash at her behavior only left me angry.

I growled again for effect.

The woman slowly glanced up, pushing her glasses up her nose to get a good look at me. Her dark blue eyes twinkled with humor as she brushed strands of hair that had fallen out of her bun off her shoulders. She turned away from me when the barman arrived and ordered a drink.

Lee

"You're in my seat?" I said, moving between her and the other patron, and leaned against the bar counter. I pushed my chest out so she could smell my aftershave; I practically bathed in the stuff.

She glanced at the floor, lifted her butt one cheek at a time, then turned to look up at me once more, narrowing her deep-blue colored eyes. "There's no name on the chair." She finished her retort with a wave of her hand, shooing me away.

I stared dumbstruck at this tiny, curvy thing with a big attitude and bunched my hands into fists, but I wouldn't hit her. I hit no one, let alone a woman, unnecessarily. I would hit back if a woman hit me first; just not as hard.

When the bartender returned he set her neat whiskey on the bar, I grabbed the glass and downed the contents.

"Hey!" she moaned, turning in the seat to look at me. "That was mine."

Once the honey liquid burned down my throat, I lifted the glass to see underneath. "There's no name, so I guess it could be anybody's." I shrugged nonchalantly, placing a note down; it was enough money to pay for the drink and a tip for the bartender. I then placed the glass on top of the money. "And don't steal the money, wench." I snapped my jaw at her as a warning.

She backed away from me with a tight smile on her face.

I pushed away from the counter and headed for my coat. Since there were no empty seats in the bar and after that altercation, I didn't feel like hanging around just to have her irritate me all evening. I thought drinking her beverage was enough punishment for stealing my chair and thought it best to get out of there while I had the last word.

As I traversed casually toward my coat I couldn't recall

from which direction she had come from, the curvy minx. I pulled on my coat and pushed the door open. Once outside, the cool air calmed me. I wiped my brow and pulled on my leather coat.

Flynn had dropped me off, but since he was no longer returning, I decided a brisk walk back to the warehouse would be better instead of calling him or a cab. It was a delightful evening for a stroll; the fresh air, stridulating insects, and a sky full of twinkling stars was what I needed to relax after that incident.

I sucked air over my teeth and caught the smell of fast-food and rain even though there were no clouds in the sky. The tension between my shoulder blades eased as I took in my surroundings in the quiet darkness, the noise of the bar long forgotten.

Being a were-leopard had its advantages; I had heightened senses, strength of fifty men, and eternal life; or until another supernatural being decided to end me. After my attack it was difficult for me to accept what I had been through and what I had become.

I'd go days not eating, not seeing friends, or leaving my room. All I wanted to do was die. I had thought my life was over. It took me a long time to realize my strengths but once I did, I used them to benefit me, and as motivation to live and move on with my life.

Not wanting to live eternity alone, I travelled the country trying to find others like me, and would accept me for who I was, and a place I could call home. Then one day I stumbled into Sterling Meadow, met Sebastian in the forest, and we clicked. Once he knew what I was and that I meant no harm, he invited me to join his leopards.

After a brief probationary period he introduced me to Léon, who offered me a job. It was pure luck that Kai and I joined the leopards at the same time, and we became friends soon thereafter.

After the attack, I was no longer allowed to prepare food for humans. And although I missed being a chef, I loved cooking for the guys at the warehouse. Every week I would try a culinary dish they had never heard of, ensuring my skills were on par even though I was never paid for it. I loved creating delectable dishes.

Deep in thought, I kicked a pebble and it skittered across the pavement and stopped at the next lamp post. The only thing I heard was my breathing and the surrounding insects.

I glanced up and saw the familiar warehouse in the distance, but before I headed in that direction, a car sped past. What happened next was quick: someone punched their hand through the window shattering it, sending shards of glass flew everywhere.

Something stung my cheek and when I wiped the area, my fingers came away with blood; but I healed quickly with little to no scarring.

The moment I saw a woman trying to climb out of the moving car, pushing her curvy body through the open window and screaming, I had to help.

Chapter Three

I recognized the curvy pint-sized woman immediately; her honey-colored hair tied in a high bun and glasses that were busy falling off her face, yet magically stayed in place.

Her forearm muscles bunched as she pulled her body out of the window, the car moving fast. Pieces of glass that didn't fall away cut her hands and arms, but she didn't seem to care. She wanted out of that death trap.

The vehicle stalled and eventually came to a stop.

She was almost out of the window when two large men exited the vehicle and tried to apprehend her. I could tell by the determination stamped on her face that she would rather die fighting than have these bozos grab her.

It would haunt me for the rest of my life if I watched them hurt her. Yes, she was a pain in the ass. But nobody deserved to be manhandled by these two.

Bozo One pulled on her bun until she screamed, loosening her hair. Then he gripped her upper arms and yanked her out of the window. Blood poured down her arms and back, but she was unperturbed as she fought him off.

Bozo Two tried to grab her legs, but she kicked him in the nuts. Then she scratched Bozo One on the cheek, but as she tore through his flesh, it knitted together just as quickly.

Vampires.

Shifters healed quickly but not *that* quick and neither did our eyes glow red, like these two knuckleheads.

"Excuse me, but do you need my help?" I asked as I approached the struggle.

"Took you long enough," said the damsel in distress.

"First tell me your name," I said, grinning. Bozo Two reached for my neck, but I sidestepped and slammed my fist into his chest. He made a wheezing sound, and I was sure dust escaped his open mouth. I waved the particles away from my face and elbowed him in the jaw. That familiar crunch sounded, followed by him spitting out a tooth and blood. "Dab your chin." I pointed at the spot he missed.

"I thought you were helping me. Instead, you're dancing with Mark."

"I love dancing." I shoved my fists into Mark's chest, sending him backwards. "The name is Lee," I grinned. "And you are?"

"Nats," she said, pushing her thumbs into Bozo One's eyes. "Sorry to do this, Simon, but I can't allow you to take me to him yet. Tell your boss to keep his panties on."

"Aargh," Simon cried, trying to pry Nats off of him, but she wasn't budging. "Just give us the item."

I applauded her for not swearing and before I could say anything else, Mark stormed into me, knocking the air out of my lungs. My abdomen burned like a swarm of bees had stung me at once. I was about to assess the damage when Mark elbowed me in the face, and all I saw was stars.

The next thing I saw was Nats running toward us, me falling to the ground, and Simon bursting into flames, then a cloud of dust. Mark was nowhere to be seen.

When I blinked, the vehicle headed toward me and stopped, and then I moved.

I felt the wound Mark had caused and my fingers came away sticky. My body would heal, slowly, but I'd be as good as new in no time.

When I moved again, I was being placed into the backseat of the car, I mumbled something to Nats about her strength. She told me to shut up and slammed the car door before I said anything else.

Chapter Four

I awoke with a start, jack-knifing out of bed and onto the floor with a loud groan. I bolted upright, glancing around and it was the living room in a stranger's house.

"Hey sleepyhead, how are you feeling?" said Nats from somewhere behind me.

"You left me on your couch," I said, inspecting my bloody and torn t-shirt and abdominal wound that had completely healed. "Typical. I save your life and you don't give me the comfort of your bed." I glanced over my right shoulder and watched her strut toward me. Narrowing my eyes, I couldn't help staring at her muscular legs and small, tight shorts. Her tight top left nothing to my imagination, and I couldn't help but think of naughty things I'd love to do to her. I cursed myself for giving in to my carnal thoughts for a woman who had done nothing but cause me trouble. I had to focus and get out of this place; wherever it was.

"You were bleeding everywhere," she said, setting a mug on the coffee table beside me. "And besides, you're a big boy and heal quickly." She winked wickedly and sat in the one-seater across from me. "How are you feeling?"

I leaned forward and peered at the dark liquid in the mug, the heavenly aroma making me salivate. I picked up the mug and enjoyed a long sip of the coffee.

"It's a good thing I didn't die for nothing then, especially since you didn't need my help. Did you, Nats?" I said after a moment of silence.

She shook her head.

"Why pretend to be in trouble?" I peered at her over the rim of the mug. She shrugged nonchalantly. I narrowed my eyes. "What do you want?" I wasn't usually suspicious of people, but this tiny bundle of dynamite had something up her sleeve. She targeted me at the bar, I was sure of it. Then the street brawl with the two bozos was possibly a dress rehearsal; like she wanted to my reaction and if I could fight.

"That mind of yours is thinking way too hard," she said, sitting back and crossing her feet on the chair.

"You knew who I was at the bar even before you stole my seat." I watched her reaction, but there was nothing. She was a pro. "Tell me the truth. Why do you need me? You seem to be capable." I started standing up and ready to leave when she stretched, placing her feet on the corner of the coffee table.

"Okay, fine. Just please stay."

"Don't lie, Nats, if that's your real name."

"My name is Natalie, but everyone calls me Nats. So yeah, it's my real name. I first went to Léon…" she left his name hanging in the air like it would mean something to me. "He said to find you."

"My boss?" The lines between my brows deepened.

She nodded, exhaling audibly. "I needed permission

from him regarding a vampire without technically involving him, 'cause you know, the council would sic someone on his ass," she grinned unconvincingly.

"What did you do?" I thumbed behind me, "back there, they mentioned an item. I gather it's something you took?"

Her shoulders dropped, and she glanced down at her hands holding her now empty mug. "It was a mistake," she said, looking up at me. "They asked me to do a job, but I should never have done it. I need your help getting the object back."

"What's the object?"

"An egg."

When she saw my expression, she added to her story. The egg in question was an ancient artifact that originated from Egypt; hidden safely with three jewels. These three jewels were important enough that, if used together, could render vampires and shifters motionless and, in effect, mortal. They believed this egg had a power similar to those jewels, but nobody knew for sure since nobody knew the extent of its power.

She added that nobody knew which story to believe because it kept changing depending on who she spoke with.

I nodded my understanding and the reason Léon had suggested she could count on me. A few years back, Léon had found and shipped those three jewels to Sterling Meadow from Egypt, but then they disappeared. Someone had almost killed Blaire Thorne because of these jewels, and Sebastian assisted her in retrieving them. Kai and I were there when they attacked the warehouse.

Long story short, Blaire had found the jewels, and the council destroyed the evil vampire who had stolen them. Nobody knew where Blaire kept the jewels, only that they were safe. She would never use them against us. Especially since she was in bed with both brothers; Léon and Sebastian.

I exhaled and nodded, recalling what had happened when Blaire put the three jewels together to activate their potent power; it had felt like insects crawling under my skin. All the hairs on my body had stood up. I felt as though I was being starved of oxygen as the pain had spread throughout my body. I wanted to die. There was nothing I could do to stop the power from eating my soul.

Blaire had only held the jewels together for a minute or two. I didn't want to know what would've happened if she kept the jewels together for longer. I shuddered at the thought of reliving it. It amazed me that the Ancient Egyptians created these weapons against supernaturals yet has mysteriously disappeared from the history books.

"You remembered something?"

"Yeah," I said, rounding my shoulders. "Let's just say the jewels work. And if the egg is anything like them," — I shuddered again, — "I don't want to feel its power. Who has the egg now?"

Natalie sat up and placed her mug on the coffee table. "He isn't a vampire or a shifter, but he could be dangerous."

"I don't like the sound of that."

She shrugged nonchalantly. "Isn't everybody dangerous?" She got to her feet and paced. "And besides, he won't like it if I ask for it back."

Chapter Five

Natalie's story was disappointing but not uncommon; she was a thief for hire and didn't care what she stole, from whom or the consequences of her actions. She was another person who lived off other people's possessions. If I were desperate for money, I might do the same, but from the looks of her apartment she wasn't battling.

Her kitchen seemed newly renovated unless she never cooked while the lounge area fitted a corner couch, that was very comfortable to sleep on, a coffee table, and a six-piece dining room table and chairs.

Her large guest bathroom featured a freestanding bath, shower, and a toilet. There were two spare bedrooms neatly decorated with the master bedroom had a walk-in closet that led to the much larger master bathroom.

Her apartment was stylish and although I wouldn't say extravagant, but it was close. I had a chance to open her closet and found a wide variety of clothing, purses, shoes, dresses, and casual wear.

What I found interesting was there were no men's

clothing or toiletries or photos anywhere. It surprised me she was unattached for someone young, beautiful, and active, unless she preferred it that way or she was a praying mantis shifter and ate her mates head after lovemaking.

I chuckled to myself as she drove and I sat shotgun. Outside the streetlights blurred past and the wind moved tree branches gently while inside the atmosphere was palpable. Natalie leaned forward and squeezed the steering wheel, her back rigid.

"Is there something else you need to tell me?" I asked, not liking her demeanor. She seemed fine before she climbed into the car, until now.

"Huh?" She glanced my way, shaking her head. "No, I told you everything."

"Then what's with this," — I pointed at her body, — "you look like you're about to strangle the steering wheel."

Natalie sat back in her seat and tried to relax. "I'm fine," she said, not elaborating.

If I had to guess, she was stressing about what lay ahead of us, but I didn't know her that well and dared not question her about it; if she said she was fine, then she was.

We passed a copse of trees, a boulder, then a sign reading Sterling Meadow Forest. Many years ago when the town was small and everybody knew everybody, it was decided that in order for shifters not to go to war with each other for a piece of land, they would separate the forest equally, ensuring each shifter group had space to hunt without getting into another were-animals way.

"Please tell me we're going to the part where leopards may roam freely?" I asked nervously. As a leopard shifter, if I entered one of the other shifters' territories without permission, they had authority to teach me a lesson and never in a fun way.

"Don't worry, it's neutral ground," she said, giving me a worrying glance.

I didn't like that one bit. They reserved the last section of the forest for the other creatures; faeries, trolls, and Blue Wolves.

Shawn was the alpha for the Wolf Pack in Sterling Meadow. He had told us about the Blue Wolves he had met while on his match-making retreat. He told us they preferred to remain hidden in the mountains. Nobody knew where they came from, but we suspect Shannon had played a part in designing their DNA in such a way that they were physically stronger than were-wolves, but they lacked a quality that kept them submissive to their cousins and in effect, kept them in the mountains.

Shannon was an evil scientist-wannabe who had tampered with Mother Nature's designs and mixed human DNA with supernatural DNA to create his own special flavor of monster. And from the stories I'd heard he had created many monsters. We didn't know where they roamed since Shannon had moved around the country during those awful years. Luckily, Blaire had destroyed Shannon. It was a dark time for her.

Natalie stopped the car, and I blinked out of my reverie. My breath caught in my throat as I craned my neck up to see the sights out of the window. There were high rocks surrounding us. I glanced over my shoulder at the narrow sand road we took and had the urge to climb out of the car and head back into town.

"I've never seen this rock formation before?" We were still in Sterling Meadow, yet I'd never come across this before and I had been everywhere in this big town; or so I thought. I opened the car door and climbed out.

Natalie was already moving toward the largest boulder

in front of us. When she reached it, she just stood and stared at it.

Slowly, I approached without interrupting her. I heard faint mumbling followed by her raising her arms as if reaching for the sky, then she pressed her hands together prayer-like. See, praying mantis. I grinned again.

The ground beneath my shoes shook, and I crouched.

Natalie remained standing, and continued praying in tongues I'd never heard before.

The enormous boulder vibrated sending tiny stones in all directions. One hit my head, I raised my hands to protect my face in case of another flying stone.

The rock formation twisted and turned, reminding me of a Transformer.

I stepped backward until I reached the car. The possibility of me surviving an attack by a huge rock-creature-thing was null. It would flatten me and the car with one swift motion of its rock fist.

"Don't worry, he won't harm you."

"He? What?"

Natalie stepped forward while the rock moved, and then she disappeared inside the rock.

"Natalie?"

"It's okay, Lee, come inside." Her voice echoing deep within.

I didn't expect that. I felt like Alice, falling down the hole. Sweat peppered my forehead. I glanced around, but there was nobody else; not a bird or insect nearby. The silence was deafening now that the rock had stopped moving.

After clearing my throat, I pushed my door closed and carefully approached the rock, nearing the spot where Natalie had disappeared from, and stepped through. The moment that happened, hard hands gripped my shoulders and lifted me up.

I screamed like a schoolgirl being attacked by bees and closed my eyes.

Laughter erupted behind me, and the hard grip relaxed.

When I opened my eyes, Natalie was standing beside a rock-man, a were-rock, whatever he was. And he blinked with rock-like eyelids.

"This is Rocco," Natalie said with humor in her eyes.

I fixed my shirt, dusting it.

Rocco grinned. Maybe. His rock features contorted in such a way that it resembled a grin. I couldn't be sure.

"Welcome," Rocco said, his voice deep and throaty. That one word echoed loud enough that I felt it in my chest.

I frowned. "Does he have the egg?" I asked, pointing at Rocco.

"No," Natalie said, shaking her head. "He's helping us."

Chapter Six

I watched these two creatures of the night talk like old pals. I didn't know why she even needed me. She had a super-rock-dude who could crush any supernatural with a flick of his thumb. His fist literally stretched out in front of him and smashed the rock in his way, making a path for us to walk.

Rocco was unbelievable. I was insanely jealous of him and hated myself for it. But I couldn't help thinking this was a waste of my time. I could be at the warehouse watching Jude and Flynn hit each other; that was more entertaining than this. Whatever this was.

After we left rock-boy's boulder home, we traversed deep inside the forest. The moon had graced us with its silver presence, lighting our way.

Rocco cleared a path for us when required while Natalie used a machete, which she removed from under her jacket, to cut the thick tree branches. She was scary, especially with that weapon in her hand. I still didn't know what kind of shifter she was. She was no vampire. But there was something strange about her. I didn't know what it was.

Lee

It felt like we'd been hiking for hours. Sweat dripped down my back, my clothing clung to my skin, and I was thirsty.

Natalie raised her fist. I stopped walking. Rocco became a... rock. The guy didn't even breathe, or at least I didn't think he needed to. He appeared to be male but made of rocks that moved like liquid mercury. It was the strangest thing. He certainly was one of a kind. And I couldn't help but frown every time he moved.

Natalie climbed up a tree like a spider monkey, and I smiled at her physical agility. I cocked my head to the side to watch her climb. In a strange, and possibly twisted way, she amazed me.

The moment she reached one of the top branches, light from a fire splashed across her face and she ducked. I think she almost crapped in her pants; her eyes were so wide all I saw was white.

I glanced at the dark green leafy fence blocking my view and listened to the low grunts and deep voices coming from the other side of the tree fence. I flinched at the harsh, grating noises; dreading the encounter.

In the three point seven seconds I knew Natalie, I'd never seen her afraid of anything, even when those two bozos attacked her. And now was no different.

I glanced at Rocco, then up at Natalie; we were three misfits attempting to reclaim an egg. We were ridiculous. Natalie's machete was the only weapon we had to defend ourselves, and I doubted whether we'd survive fighting many supernaturals at once; especially those grunting on the other side of the fence. I side-eyed Rocco, perhaps five supernaturals each was the maximum.

I wondered if Natalie had a flamethrower in her bra since that machete seemed to come out of nowhere. I chuckled at the thought and felt the heavy gaze from above. When I glanced up, she silently shushed me. I shrugged. My smile still on my face.

Nats could see the village on the other side of the tree fence, and stayed in an awkward crouch on the tree branch as she watched. Her lips moved as if she was speaking with someone, but I couldn't hear her words. I wondered whether she was counting how many we needed to kill.

I hated hurting others unnecessarily and wondered whether this was a good idea. I should've phoned Léon to ask if this chick was legit. She knew enough about me, and I believed her.

I sighed wearily. Next time I had to do a thorough check... if we survived.

Rocco moved quietly toward the fence where he parted leaves, revealing vines holding the structure together. Through the vines, I caught movement and a fire burning.

I passed him and walked along the edge of the fence but couldn't find a gate or another way inside.

A twig snapped. I froze. When nothing else happened, I slowly turned to my left and Natalie waved me back.

"Beyond that fence are trolls," she whispered.

I shuddered involuntarily. I didn't like trolls. They were disgusting, vile, and terribly powerful creatures. I was right; we were going to die.

"We won't die," Natalie said, her brows knitting together.

"Did you just read my mind?" I asked, pointing a finger at her.

She stared at me, ignoring my question.

Now I really didn't know what type of supernatural creature she was.

"I always have a contingency plan." She glanced at

Rocco. I wondered if he was going to smash them all to dust.

"How can I trust you if you can't answer a simple question?" I glared at her, folding my arms.

"What I am is not important, Lee. It's important that we get the egg back." She bit her lip and didn't blink; her eyes glistening in the moonlight.

"Then answer me this. Why did you need me to tag along? You two," — I pointed at Rocco and then at her, — "seem to have everything planned perfectly."

"I need you to hold the egg."

"I will become mortal. Who will protect me?"

She smiled slyly. I didn't like that smile. Any kind of smile from her left me on edge.

"Ready?"

"Yes," Rocco said.

"No," I mumbled.

Chapter Seven

I fought my beast from shoving its toothy jaw through my face and latching onto Natalie's arm. I didn't appreciate the secrecy about this so-called mission. What she had told me was the truth, but she omitted most of the information.

"I promise I'll tell you everything once we have the egg. I don't see why I need to go into the detail now." Natalie glanced nervously at the wooden fence. "Clear your head and let's get this over and done with." She patted my shoulder and squeezed.

Rocco walked on my right, and he too draped a heavy, rocky arm around my shoulders and brought me in for a manly hug, one where we didn't touch too much, yet he still wanted to show he cared. I pushed him away.

"Fine," I said, pointing the same finger at her. "But you have to tell everything if we survive this."

"I promise," she said, gripping my finger and lowering it. "Now stand down before you shoot someone with that finger."

"Ha, she made a funny." I pulled my hand away from

her and stood on the other side of Rocco, ensuring he stayed in the middle.

She smiled.

I shook out my arms and rounded my shoulders. "Do you need my beast to say hello?" I asked, knowing my leopard's eyes were shining brightly, casting her dark blue eyes in light. I frowned when I spotted a nictitating eyelid. She read minds, had super strength, and a second eyelid reminding me of a reptile. My head hurt wondering what kind of supernatural she was.

She stared at me for a heartbeat. Her somber expression chiseling at my heartstrings. I didn't know her well, but from the sorrow in her eyes, I might need tissues when she decided to tell me her story, and I trusted her to tell me everything when all this was over.

"Yes, we'll need your beast. Then, when they give me the egg, I'll hand you your clothing. It's up to you to keep the egg safe. Please, Lee, you're the only one who can do this for me. For us." She glanced nervously at Rocco again.

"Fine," I grumbled.

In the short time we had known each other, I never sensed dishonesty but she wasn't telling me everything, and I was sure she had a reason. But right now, she needed my help, and as much as I wanted to I couldn't say no.

I kicked off my shoes, removed my shirt, and stripped down to my birthday suit. When I noticed Natalie staring, I grinned. Slowly, I folded my clothing, handing the bundle to her. She couldn't tear her eyes away from my body as she clutched my clothes to her chest.

I didn't shift into my beast immediately because I enjoyed watching her squirm and trying not to stare at me. It relieved me to know she still had a human side, and it was possible to embarrass her, just like any woman.

"Um, please, for the love of the gods, change already," she grumbled, and turned around. "Once you're, ah," — she glanced over her shoulder, her eyes raking up and down my body, — "um." She shook her head and rubbed her eyes, forcing them closed with her free hand. "When you're in form, Rocco will open the fence for us."

"Cool," I said, and leaped into the air. I was not a natural born were-leopard; my shift wasn't without pain; it wasn't as painful as the first time, but it got easier each time. I wasn't as strong as those naturally born, but I was determined enough to make up for my shortcoming with my wit, charm, and good looks.

By the time I landed on the ground, I was in my beast's form; a large, fluffy, snow-leopard.

Natalie glanced down at me, her eyes wide as saucers, and her mouth wide open.

"Stop drooling over me," I mumbled the words through my toothy jaw, but she could still understand me.

Natalie closed her mouth and blinked. Her right hand clutched at her chest while her left hand reached for my back. Slowly, she combed her fingers through my coat.

"You're so soft," she whispered, crouching lower. She wrapped her arms around my neck and with her head against mine, near enough to my muzzle, I smelled her. I caught all different types of scents; soap, perfume, and her, but there was another scent I recognized. I couldn't smell as well in my human form, but in my beast, I smelled everything.

My heart rate sped up. Heat from her hands against my body was a comfort as she continued rubbing the fur on my back, sides, and against my chest. I wanted to purr.

Someone cleared their throat. The ground vibrated beneath my feet, and Rocco stood beside Natalie. "I hate to interrupt whatever you're doing, but we have a time limit here." Rocco tapped his naked rock-wrist for effect.

Natalie rubbed her nose against my bony cheek and kissed me. It was just a quick peck, but it felt more than that to me. Something happened between us those few seconds and I couldn't understand it; but I felt it—the effects lingering around my chest.

"Let's do this," Natalie said, dusting imaginary sand off her clothing and stood. She reached for the fence and leaned against it. She nodded and Rocco walked through the thick tree fence like it was spaghetti.

Once Rocco was through, Natalie went next, and I brought up the rear. We stood beside each other near the bonfire we had seen earlier and sitting around the flames were at least a hundred trolls, each with an axe in hand.

Chapter Eight

I heard Rocco swallow. It sounded excruciatingly painful.

"Uh, where's Elwyn?" Natalie asked, stepping forward. "We only want what's rightfully ours."

"Who dares break into our village at this godly hour? We should destroy you for that alone!" Boomed a voice lost in the sea of large, brown and green bodies.

Heavy footsteps neared, and the ocean of trolls parted.

His skin was darker than the others, too, with large tusks extending from his mouth, and two on each side near his bottom lip. He covered his large muscular arms and chest in a variety of smaller tusks and severed ears on strings, while a fur loincloth covered his front.

He towered over Natalie. The flames of the fire bathed his face in sinister light, making him look scarier than he was. Or I hoped he wasn't as scary as he looked.

I was nervous. I could imagine how Natalie felt, but she didn't show fear; she revealed no emotion. She seemed immune.

Natalie raised her head and held her position. "Elwyn,

please. You know the egg doesn't belong to you. Please, may I have it back?" She held out her hand, palm facing upward.

Elwyn laughed; that rumbling sound came from deep within his chest. He bunched his hands into fists and grunted.

"I paid you for it, Nats. It's poor form to ask for the item back. You know this. There are rules we follow," he said in an ominous tone.

"I know…" her shoulders sagged, and she closed her eyes, exhaling. "I should never have agreed to it. But I didn't know." When she opened them again, the second eyelid moved. Elwyn noticed and stepped backward. "I'm sorry," she added quickly, rushing to his aid, but he raised both arms, letting her know not to come any closer.

"What are you, Natalie?" Elwyn said, shaking his head. "Please don't hurt my people." He pushed those closest to him back and spoke in a language I'd never heard before. They all retreated to their huts except twenty warriors who remained behind to protect their leader.

Natalie raised her hands. "I don't want to hurt you or your people. I come in peace. A deal is a deal and in exchange for the egg, I'm giving you Rocco."

I glanced at Rocco; my leopard jaw opening wide.

Rocco stepped forward and bowed respectfully.

"Why would you trade your friend?" Elwyn asked, his brows knitting together.

"Because I value our relationship and want it to continue in a healthy manner," she said with sincerity. "I mean it when I say I don't want to hurt your people, Elwyn. I don't, but I will if I have to. You know I will. Please… please give me the egg," she pleaded.

Elwyn grunted. He spoke in his native tongue and a troll

ran somewhere deep within the village. Elwyn stared wordlessly at Natalie, unimpressed.

"What were they going to do with the egg?" I asked the question burning.

"It heals our people. But it destroys vampires," Elwyn answered, but continued staring at Natalie with disdain. "At least we used it." His emotionless tone felt like blades down my spine.

The four minutes it took for the troll to return with the egg were the longest four minutes of my life. It physically hurt me to watch Natalie and Elwyn glare at each other, willing the other to die a violent death.

The troll handed the cloth wrapped egg to Elwyn, who hesitantly handed it to Natalie.

Rocco placed a hard hand on Natalie's shoulder before stepping closer to Elwyn. He did not look back at her. One troll led Rocco away, and he didn't look back then either.

I would rather fight where there was blood and teeth being removed than watch this depressing display. I barely knew Rocco, and it hurt to watch him leave; to be given up so easily. And from what I understood, he and Natalie were close friends. Yet she swapped him like an object for her personal gain. It was a cold, heartless move. She was cruel. There weren't even tears in her cold, dry eyes.

I didn't want to stay here any longer. The quicker I changed and kept the egg safe, the sooner I could leave and go home.

Chapter Nine

Once we had the egg and I was dressed, we hiked back to Natalie's car in silence. By the time we reached her vehicle, the sun had already graced us with its beating heat. The birds sang and various creatures scuttled across the forest grounds. The world continued as if we didn't swap a rockman for an egg.

I side-eyed Natalie; either she was an excellent actor or handing over her friend didn't faze her one bit.

I shook my head in disgust as I opened the car door.

"I know what you're thinking, Lee. You don't understand—"

"Then tell me what's going on, because right now you seem like a cold-hearted bitch." I spat the words out with such hate, I hoped it hurt.

Her expression changed, like I'd just slapped her. She blinked back tears and swallowed hard. "You don't understand..." her voice broke, and she glanced at her feet, then at a tree on her other side. When she looked at me again, tears streamed down her face. "Come with and see for yourself."

I climbed into the car. "Fine, but no more human exchanges."

She responded by starting the engine and pulling out onto the quiet road.

For miles, silence filled the space. The purr of the engine kept my mind from wandering as I gazed out of the window at the scenery blurring past.

Natalie drove through Sterling Meadow and carried on driving. I knew who we were going to see when I saw the sign for Krystal Creek. There was only one vampire living here, and I wasn't looking forward to the encounter.

I rubbed against the side of the egg, the engraved pattern that wound around the egg and the hieroglyphics I couldn't decipher. The more I rubbed the egg, the hairs on my forearms stood on end. I shuddered and the hairs on my entire body stood up.

"Would I die if you had an accident right now?" I asked, holding on to the fragile artifact.

Natalie glanced at me quickly before turning her attention back to the road. "From what I understand, it affects vampires. We suspect it could affect shifters, but nobody knows for sure." She shrugged. "To be honest, I don't feel the pull of its power. Do you?"

"Ah, so you are a shifter?"

Her smile reached her eyes. When she looked at me again, her dark blue eyes bled to swamp green, and her forked tongue tasted the air. A wave of scales spread across her cheek and down her neck before receding again.

I blinked at her. My frown deepened. I didn't know what shifter she was. "Crocodile?"

"Close," she grinned. "Komodo dragon."

"No shit?"

"No shit."

My smile split my face in two. "I've never heard of Komodo dragon shifters before. I know of the Komodo dragon reptile, but..." I left my sentence hanging, prompting her to explain.

She cleared her throat and squeezed the steering wheel.

I sensed hesitation. That whatever had happened was bad, and for someone as tough as her, it had to be extreme.

"Everybody knows about Shannon?"

"Yes," I said, nodding. "He's the evil scientist who combined shifter and human DNA with whatever else and created his own private army."

"Yes, well, he created us, my sister and me, in the same laboratory Blaire killed him in." That explained why her scent was so familiar. I'd smelled it on Blaire. I should've recognized it.

She cleared her throat and blinked. "We escaped before his demise and hid here," — she nodded toward the "Krystal Creek" sign as we drove past it, — "we first stayed with a lovely young couple. But when they realized we were shifters and a potential threat to their infant son, they kicked us out. That's when I found a job working for the only vampire in town."

"Ian."

"Yes, Ian."

"And that's why you came to Léon?" Ian used to be part of Léon's kiss until Blaire came along and disrupted everything for the best, but some vampires would argue that fact. Like Ian.

She nodded, avoiding my gaze.

I suspected Ian was more than just her employer. Ian was one of those exceptionally good-looking vampires who made men feel insignificant the moment they met him.

I'd heard Elena, one of Léon's were-rat security guards, express how hypnotic Ian's blue eyes were and she'd give her left foot to have one night with him.

My beast growled.

Natalie glanced my way, a shocked expression. "What's wrong?"

"So, are you and Ian an item?"

"No!" she yelled. "We, uh, we were, but then…," — she shook her head, — "it's complicated."

I shoved my angry beast down. Natalie and I weren't an item and I had no right to be mad at her or Ian. I was not the jealous type, but if she were mine… let's just say I protected to the death what belonged to me. She would never be my possession, she would be my mate, my equal, my best friend, my lover. But she was not my mate. She was nothing of mine and nothing to my beast.

I shook my head. I was thinking of things that meant nothing. They weren't reality and I had no right to claim her.

I unclenched my jaw and folded my arms, the egg resting carefully on my lap.

The air inside the car became unbreathable. Natalie sensed it too and opened a window at the same time I did.

As I opened my mouth to say something, the car stopped outside a large house with green walls.

Chapter Ten

"Aren't we early?" I asked, glancing at the sun and then at the awful, green-colored house.

She sighed audibly. "Yes, Ian is down for the day, but I live here. Besides, this is where I must return the egg."

I glanced at the beautifully crafted egg. "Why would you steal from Ian? And why would Ian, a vampire, want the egg in his house if it was bad for him?"

She ignored my questions and opened the front door. "Come on, let me show you." She left the door open as she entered the large house and disappeared into the darkness.

I exhaled, glanced down at the egg in my hands, and traversed the path inside the bowels of the green home.

I gently closed the front door behind me, because the last thing I wanted to do was wake the vampire, and followed the sounds of Natalie in the kitchen. When I entered, she placed raw cubed meat into a silver bowl and headed toward the basement door on the other side of the kitchen.

Natalie disappeared down the basement stairs while I

remained at the top with my hand on the door handle, not wanting to venture down there, yet curious. The smell of the dank room and rotten meat smacked me in the face and stole my breath away.

I covered my mouth with my hand but it was futile. My eyes watered as I breathed through my nose. No matter what I tried it didn't lesson the stench.

"What's taking you so long?" Natalie called from down below.

Not wanting to seem like a wimp, I traversed down the uneven stairs carefully with one hand against the uneven wall and the other still covering my mouth and nose.

The father down I went, the thicker the darkness became. When I finally reached the bottom of the stairs I stayed on the last step watching the only light swing from side to side, highlighting parts of the basement as it moved. I could do nothing but stare open-mouthed.

"What the hell is going on?" I said, stepping onto the basement floor and staying there. My eyes danced across the gloomy room as I took everything in; the ominous cage, the carcass, rotten meat in heaps on the floor, and dried blood. So much blood. It's as if the walls and floors were painted in the coagulating liquid.

It hissed.

I glanced at the creature, and its dark eyes were on me. Its forked tongue tasted the air—tasted me—and swished its large, thick tail from side to side. It blinked; the nictitating eyelid moved. It didn't tear its eyes away from me, even when Natalie climbed inside the cage.

"Wait—" I started, needing to protect her. But the moment the word left my mouth, it was too late. The creature charged at the cage; the sound deafening as it struck the bars, bending them outward. It shook its head, its eyes on me again, and it backed up. It wanted to charge again, break free and eat me.

"No, Penn! Stop!" Natalie yelled, throwing the bowl of raw meat on the ground and stood in front of the creature, blocking her view of me. "No! He's a friend. He helped us. Now behave." Natalie stepped away from Penn and pointed at me. "This is Lee. He's a friend. Do not eat him!"

Natalie crouched and scooped the chunks of meat in the bowl again and placed it near Penn. "Sorry breakfast is late. And besides," — she glanced at me, — "I don't think he would taste nice, anyway. He's too skinny for you," she said, winking wickedly. "Just look, there's hardly any muscle. He's just skin and bone." She lied; I was nothing but muscle.

Natalie rubbed Penn's head while she ate. "There we go. See, isn't that tastier," Natalie said, still rubbing Penn's head. "You would just choke on him anyway."

I wanted to chuckle but thought it best to keep quiet and not distract the angry, oversized creature while she ate.

When Natalie was content Penn wouldn't charge the cage again, she exited and locked it behind her. She stood beside me and stared at Penn.

"I'm sure you've gathered that Penn is my sister," she said sadly. "The one night I allow her to go out alone with friends she gets into trouble. They crossed paths with a witch who hates shifters and cursed Penn and her three friends."

When Natalie glanced at me, I saw the pain of what had happened reflect in her eyes. The sadness. The regret.

"It happened about a year ago," she said, nodding in Penn's direction. "They captured and killed her friends because they went rogue, rabid, completely mental." She paused, the silence like shards of glass down my back. "The curse stopped them from changing back into their human form and I'm sure you're aware, any shifter who stays in their beast for a really long time gets loopy." She tried for humor and I smiled, but I could tell it hurt her to speak about what had happened.

"And after a year you've kept her from going full animal." I stated. I'd heard of a handful of shifters who, after some time in their beast form, remained like that. They usually disappeared for fear of being hunted and destroyed. Whether they survived the wild of the forest, nobody know.

"Ian thinks it's because I'm her sister and can still communicate with her telepathically. Some days are harder and I need to shout at her, like today, but the important thing is she hears me, understands me and doesn't stay lost within herself. My sister is still there." She smiled sadly. "I love you, Penn," Natalie shouted.

Penn stopped chewing and glanced up. She hissed, her forked tongue tasted the air again, and she continued eating.

"You think the egg can somehow help her, and that's why Rocco offered himself to the trolls."

She nodded, blinking back tears. "I told him we could find another way, that he didn't have to do it. But he wouldn't hear it. He knew the trolls couldn't say no to a supernatural like him. And he still gave his life for hers. I owe him my life."

Her revelation opened my eyes to her true intentions, and it left me miserable for thinking she was a cold heartless asshole. I regretted saying that to her, but there were things still bothering me.

"There are a few things troubling me about the egg—"

"The egg heals trolls. We hope it can heal Penn," she said. "Ian found a witch who can try to lift the curse." She exhaled a frustrated breath. "When I first stole the egg, I didn't know what it was until Ian said we needed it. And I didn't steal it from Ian. I stole it from one of his lesser vampires, but because Ian is a master and his friend, I needed to bring it here—on mutual ground and Ian will pay the vampire in gold. Anyway, it's a mess. What's important is I have it and the witch should be here soon to perform the ritual."

"Don't worry, I understand; the trolls commissioned you to get the egg. You didn't know the genuine quality of the object until after you handed it to the trolls. And because you need it to heal Penn, Rocco offered himself. And since you stole from a vampire, Ian needs to save face but still help you." I breathed, glancing between Penn and Natalie.

"What?" Natalie wanted to say more but didn't.

"Ian—"

"What about me?" boomed a deep voice behind us, followed by footsteps.

"You didn't have to send the guys to fetch me, Ian. You know I'll do what needs doing."

"I know my dear, but I had to make sure," Ian said, descending the stairs. It looked like he floated down with his hands away from his sides, reminding me of a king presenting himself. I almost rolled my eyes. "I couldn't have you running around doing your own thing again. Now I must replace the men you destroyed." He glanced down at me, his lips curling upward in disgust. "But you made it back in time, and you brought one of Léon's man-boys," Ian said with an outstretched hand. "Hand it over."

"Are you sure? It might make you mortal and I could bite your head off." I snapped, keeping the egg in my possession.

"It's all tales. The egg will do no such thing. Now hand

it over, boy," Ian demanded, wiggling his fingers. "And tell your master he owes me money." Ian grabbed the egg out of my hand and headed upstairs. "Come, darling, the witch is waiting."

I mouthed the word 'darling', asking Natalie a silent question.

Natalie lowered her head in shame and followed Ian up the stairs.

I didn't like where this was heading, and neither did my beast.

Chapter Eleven

I leaned against the wall with my arms folded, and pressing my head into the wall to feel pain; anything to get my mind off everything. Anger radiated off of me and I didn't care who felt it. I didn't like what I was seeing, and knew Penn would be just as upset if she were here witnessing the same thing.

The witch prepared the potion using the contents of the egg; whatever was inside looked thick and lumpy. Then she crushed the shell and mixed that in, too. She spat words that left me tongue tied, and I felt the pull of the spell's power.

But that wasn't what made me angry.

Natalie was sitting on Ian's lap, whispering sweet nothings to each other. His hands were all over her body and she allowed him to touch her that way even with me staring. I think Ian enjoyed giving me a show while Natalie took pleasure in having him paw at her.

I fisted my hands and readied to smash my way through every wall in this ugly, green-colored house. But I had to curb my frustration; she wasn't mine and she was not my mate. I had no right to feel this way and couldn't understand why; these feelings were wrong; they meant nothing. Yet...

Beast growled inside my head. He thought Natalie could be ours. He wanted her to be ours.

"If you don't need me anymore," I said loudly so they could hear me over their stupid whispering. "Do you think you could take me back to Sterling Meadow?"

"You'll stay the night," Ian stated. "I want to make sure the egg works for my darling's little sister. If not, I need you to help Nats get the next thing."

"Why me? Can't you be the vampire of the hour and help your *darling* out?" I spat out the words like venom. Then waited for the wrath of the vampire to strike with a flick of his wrist. But all Ian did was laugh.

"You're funny, boy. No, I am Master Vampire of Krystal Creek. I can't go anywhere. You're a boy-servant, so that's what you'll do. Serve. If not, I will tell Léon you disobeyed me, and I will demand your head." Ian glanced at me over Natalie's head, his piercing blue eyes a stern warning.

Asshole.

But I'd keep my opinions to myself. Natalie would turn on me in a heartbeat.

"If you don't need me I'll be outside. I need fresh air," I said, pushing away from the wall. I traversed through the house and out the back door. Once the cool evening wind caressed my face, and the smell of rain assaulted my olfactory senses, I relaxed.

The anger I held onto rolled off of me and I shook out my arms. I crossed the yard and traversed down a narrow path toward the river that ran past the vampire's house and, most likely, through the small town.

The tree branches moved as the wind blew through

them; making them sway and wave, reminding me of the mountains near Sterling Meadow.

"I don't want to be with him," Natalie whispered behind me.

I jumped, almost hitting her in the face with my head. "Christ, I didn't hear you sneak up on me?"

She grinned. I smiled back at her. Then I remembered I was angry with her and scowled.

"Oh, stop it." She smacked my shoulder. "You're just jealous because you're a stomper. I can teach you to move stealthily. Then you can sneak up on anyone."

I rolled my eyes. "Why?" I asked. That one word was sufficient.

"I'd do anything to get my sister back, Lee. Anything. I know Ian. He'll soon grow tired of me; or I'll make sure of it." She sighed and closed the gap. Her face was so close to mine that I felt her hot breath against my cheek. "I don't even like him," she whispered. "I have do it this."

When I turned my face to meet hers our lips were so close I only needed to lean slightly forward and we'd touch. My eyes flittered from her mouth to her eyes and the blue of her irises reminded me of icebergs.

"There are many witches we could ask for help. You don't have to count on him to do anything for you," I whispered.

She closed her eyes as if counting to a hundred. When she opened them again, I caught a hint of humor. "I have already promised it. You know how vampires are."

I nodded my understanding and stepped away from her. Once you promise anything to a vampire, you're bound to that promise until it's fulfilled. It's like making a deal with a lesser devil.

"Thank you for caring." Her smile reached her eyes. "It

means the world to me." She stepped closer and squeezed my arm but didn't let go.

I glanced over her head at the house, grateful the trees providing us with privacy. I didn't think. I reacted. I cupped her face and kissed her, and she hungrily kissed back. Her lips were soft against mine. Her body pressed against me, and I felt her soft curves. Our hands roaming, touching the other, and she felt so good against me.

A door slammed somewhere inside the house. I reluctantly let her go.

Her eyes were still closed when her hand reached for her face, and she touched her lips. When she opened her eyes, her smile widened.

"Natalie!" Ian yelled. He stood near the back door with his hands on his hips, searching for her.

"Got to go—"

"Wait, can we talk about this?"

"Later," she whispered, kissed me one last time, and ran away.

Chapter Twelve

I stood back and watched the witch do her thing with Natalie close by.

Penn swished her large tail, not allowing anyone near her, including her sister.

"Let me tranquilize her—" Ian started saying.

"No!" Natalie shook her head. "Just give her a chance." She scowled at Ian. I smiled inside. Her eyes flitted from Ian to me and back to him. I was sure he saw it but neglected to mention it.

"Fine, but understand if she hurts you, I will destroy her."

"Please, Ian. I beg of you, go wait for me upstairs. We'll be fine, and besides, Lee can help me if I need it."

Ian raised his head and glared down at me like I was bubblegum stuck under his shoe. I stared back. I knew the risk; staring into a vampire's eyes could get my head chopped off, or worse, caught under his spell. But I didn't care, I was ready to fight; I'd had enough of him.

Ian brushed past me, slamming his shoulder into mine.

He wanted me to start a fight he knew I'd never win, but I wouldn't give him the satisfaction. I allowed his abuse, because it would only last a minute or two then he'd grow bored and leave me alone.

When he realized I wouldn't retaliate, he stomped up the stairs and slammed the door behind him.

I shrugged and approached the cage. I didn't have time for him. If he wanted to fight he would have to start it.

Penn had been staring at me the entire time and I caught the glint in her swamp-green colored eyes.

I tipped my head slightly. I hated Ian as much as she did. When I smiled, Penn tasted the air with her forked tongue.

"Do it now, child," the witch croaked, pointing a crooked finger at Natalie. She reminded me of the witch from Hansel and Gretel. I wondered…

"Lee," Nats said, disrupting my thoughts. "Come help me, please." She pointed at the open cage door.

"Hopefully, she doesn't bite my ass," I grumbled, reaching for the cage.

"She won't."

"You best be right." I opened the cage door and stepped inside.

The witch moved out of my way, handing me the solution.

Natalie crouched near Penn's toothy jaw and scratched underneath. "It's okay, sister. We'll get you back to your old self in no time."

Penn hissed and swished her tail.

My veins filled with ice as I imagined the pain from the venom of Penn's bite. But she didn't attack, instead she just stared at me hungrily.

Natalie raised her open hand.

Lee

I placed the solution carefully into her palm and crouched beside her. If Penn was going to bite me, she would've done so already, but I'd remain cautious.

Penn blinked. Her swampy-green colored eyes not leaving mine. She opened her mouth, hissed, and allowed Natalie to pour the concoction into her mouth.

Penn hissed and backed away, inflating her throat. Her hissing became louder as the solution took its hold on her. She shook her enormous head, still hissing. Her solid body bumped up against the sides of the wall then the cage, shaking it. If she had space, I was sure she'd run away.

I suspected it tasted awful, and hoped it healed her.

Penn continued the hissing and bumping against the sides of the wall and cage, drawing blood.

Natalie wanted to go to her sister to comfort her but knew better, she'd only get injured and that was bad for everyone.

Penn knocked her head hard against the wall, leaving her momentarily stunned. She stood still for a moment, unseeing then collapsed to the ground with a loud thud. Natalie fell with her, trying desperately to reach for her sister.

"Give her space," I said, pulling Natalie back. "There isn't anything you can do for her now except wait. But wait here." I pointed at a spot near my foot and away from Penn where she couldn't hurt Natalie.

Natalie complied, sitting near my feet while I caressed the top of her head. After a moment she relaxed and leaned her head against my thigh.

Penn's icky green colored eyes sparkled yellow.

Natalie flinched.

I grabbed Natalie's head to stop her from crawling to Penn.

Penn moaned and hissed as she fought the poison coursing through her veins. I hoped the concoction worked to eradicate the witch's curse, and she shifted back into her human self.

Penn's scales moved, reflecting light, and hope fluttered in my chest. I imagined how relieved Natalie felt, but when Penn didn't change, my hope shattered on the floor like shards of glass.

Penn didn't move. I barely saw her breathe.

"What? No, what have you done, witch? What did you do to my sister?" Natalie cried, pushing away from me, and reached for her sister. "No," she mumbled, holding onto Penn's lifeless head. "No…"

I backed away, nudging the witch to move faster. Natalie needed time alone, time to mourn the loss of her sister. And she would need time before she could move forward; if she didn't go through the stages of grief, she'd turn into a different kind of monster.

"Call me if you need me," I said, standing at the foot of the stairs. I doubted she heard me as I watched her cry silently with her sister's reptilian corpse.

Death was cruel, particularly to those left behind to pick up the pieces. Nobody wanted to deal with the aftereffects of losing a loved one, or to fill the void they left.

I climbed the steps slowly in case Natalie needed me to come back down, but she didn't call out. When I reached the top of the stairs, I heard her faint sobbing.

I wanted to take her pain away, to hold her tightly, and to let her know I was there for her. That I understood her loss, and if she needed to punch something, she could hit me, and I would comfort her afterwards. Then we could stand at the top of a hill and scream our pain into the wind.

Then we would do it all over again. And if she wanted, I would remain by her side for as long as she needed me.

"Is the bitch dead?" Ian boomed behind me, making me flinch. I spun around and faced his chest. The asshole was tall for a vampire. When I didn't answer, he stepped backward and stared at me like I was a steak he wanted to devour. "Well, is she?"

"What the hell is wrong with you? Natalie's sister just died, and you speak about her like that."

"I only care about Natalie, servant, and her sister was always in the way."

I closed my mouth and took a step back, closing the basement door. I didn't want Natalie to hear Ian spew vile words about her sister. Not now, in any case. I was sure he'd reveal his true self to her in time, if he hadn't already done so.

I narrowed my eyes at the vampire. "Does Léon know of your underhanded machinations?"

"What I do in Krystal Creek is none of his business," he scoffed. He turned to leave when I jumped onto his back, digging my partially shifted claws into his neck.

Chapter Thirteen

Ian tried to throw me off, but I clung to him, digging my claws deeper into his soft vampire flesh. He roared frustratingly when he realized I wasn't going anywhere.

I wrapped my legs around his waist and squeezed. Then I removed my right claw from his neck and stabbed my sharp fingernails into the soft parts of his abdomen.

"Argh!" Ian roared. "I'm going to kill you, shifter." Ian gripped my shoulders and flipped me over his head and off his back.

I detached myself from his tender flesh and scooted away from him.

"Your fucking nails are sharp," Ian shrieked, pulling a broken nail out of his chest. I winced at the sight, realizing my index fingernail had torn. He flicked the nail away and turned his red gaze on me; I was going to die, and he'd ensure it would be painful.

I couldn't outrun him; he'd fly into me and knock me into next week. So I did what I thought best; I stood gracefully and accepted my fate. I said I'd fight him, so that's what I'd do.

With one foot slightly behind me, I braced for an attack. I raised my hands, protecting my face. Ian flew into me, sending me into the far side of the kitchen wall. I landed with a loud thud and quickly climbed to my feet. The last thing I needed was a blindsided attack and him removing my head.

When the lights went out, I groaned. "No fair, bat, I can't see you." But I heard him. I closed my eyes and concentrated. I needed my beast. My beast was better at everything.

I brought my beast to the front, shredded my clothing during the change, and padded across the kitchen floor like I wasn't about to be destroyed by a bloodsucker.

When I heard movement in the corner of the kitchen ceiling, I stopped and stared up at the vampire hiding. He was desperately trying to avoid the were-leopard hunting him, but I saw his dark shadow.

Ian's heart rate sped up; which was unnerving since vampire hearts stopped beating the moment they became the undead. Then silence filled the air. He had probably realized he'd jump started his heart somehow and needed to calm down to avoid detection.

The kitchen corner darkened as the vampire disappeared from the spot. I couldn't hear him anymore and the blackness of the kitchen spread throughout. I no longer saw the kitchen counter, the stove, or the fridge. The dark inkiness enveloped me, threatening to suffocate me.

My hackles raised. I growled, turning slightly to my right, coming face-to-face with red eyes. I bolted for him, biting something bony and meaty.

Ian struck me two, three times, trying to dislodge my

jaw from his arm, but I bit down harder. Crunching sounded, followed by him screaming and kicking me away.

I yelped from the impact. The kitchen brightened. I blinked leopard eyes, watching Ian's forearm heal.

He screamed as he darted for me, crashing into me, and sending us through the wall and into the backyard.

An owl hooted, flying past us. Ian opened his fanged mouth and bit into my shoulder. I scratched his jaw, but he didn't let go. I scratched again, almost tearing his jaw from his face. That caught his attention, and he unlatched himself from me.

The moment he backed away, his jaw healed and he readied himself for another attack. Hate filled his features, and I suspected he'd take great pleasure in tearing into my soft belly.

I wanted this fight to end, but I didn't want to die. I stood my ground and waited for his assault.

Ian rounded his shoulders and pushed away from the tree. But he didn't get far. The largest Komodo dragon I'd ever seen walked dangerously between us, blocking his path, and swishing her tail. I could only assume it was Natalie protecting me. She was easily twice the size of me and her tail twice as long.

She was a formidable force, and I never wanted to piss her off.

Her green and dark brown scaly skin shimmered in the moonlight as her long tail swished back and forth. Her bright yellow eyes filled with fury, and Ian was her target.

She snapped her jaw. The sound was ear-piercing, but it was her venom I'd be most worried about.

"That's enough, Ian. I'm not in the mood to kill anyone tonight but I will if I have to. Just leave Lee alone," she said clearly.

Ian was not happy. It looked like he wanted to rip Natalie in two but thought otherwise. Her bite would maim him, and I was sure her claws would easily remove his head; rendering him true dead.

Ian leaned against the tree and closed his eyes, his healed jaw muscles twitching. When he opened his eyes, he glared daggers at her.

Noises from the kitchen caught our attention. The back door opened, followed by an emaciated woman stopping on the steps. Penn. She didn't look pleased.

"Darling, you're okay," Ian said pleasantly, slowly moving in the direction of the house.

I turned my head in time to see Natalie strike. She gripped his ankle with her talons on her right claw, then her left claw removed his right leg just above his knee. When he fell, she crawled on top of him and bit into his neck before he realized what had just happened.

I didn't want to intervene. Natalie had a reason to attack him, and I suspected Ian had something to do with Penn's curse to begin with.

Natalie gnawed at Ian's neck, blood spraying everywhere, until his head popped off. He burst into angry flames, his ashes resting on the ground beneath Natalie's large, scaly body.

When it was all over, Natalie changed back into her human form. It was difficult to watch her shift back; her pain-filled screams. The sounds of her broken bones reforming and her muscles tearing took me back to my first change after my attack. The only difference, Natalie felt the pain every time she shifted. I only experienced that level of pain and discomfort once.

One look at her expression and I knew she suffered each time. It really was a curse for her.

Chapter Fourteen

I pulled the robe tighter around my body and shivered when a gust of wind blew through the enormous hole in the wall.

Natalie kept smirking at the pink item I used to cover my body with.

I growled.

Penn kicked my shin under the kitchen table.

"Ow!" I cried, rubbing my leg. "Uncalled for," I quipped, then pointed at Natalie. "Léon is going to have my head for what you've done."

"Don't worry so much, Lee," she said, patting my knee in a patronizing way. "I made sure everything would be fine." Her eyes flitted to the corner of the kitchen where Ian had hidden, and I frowned. I wondered if Natalie had cameras installed.

"So anyway," — Penn continued, — "before I was so rudely interrupted." She rolled her eyes and smiled. She was making fun of me, and I couldn't help but grin. "When Ian told me where to go, I didn't think it was suspicious, until that witch found us. A coincidence, my ass. I know he sent her to get rid of me," Penn grumbled.

Natalie nodded, stood up and hugged her sister, who remained seated. "He's gone now," she whispered, then kissed the top of her sister's head. When she looked up, she added, "And I will explain everything to Léon. Don't worry your pretty little head."

I didn't want a woman fighting my battles for me, but I also didn't want to fight with Natalie yet. When we arrive in Sterling Meadow, I would speak with Léon before she had the chance.

Yes, Natalie killed Ian, but I knew better and should've stopped her. Ian was one of Léon's vampires. My job as Léon's employee was to protect those in his kiss, and I didn't.

I shrugged. There was nothing I could do except explain the situation and hope for the best.

"Don't look so worried, Lee," Natalie said, bringing me out of my thoughts. "I'm just glad my sister is back. The consequences can wait."

"I need new clothes." I pulled on the robe.

The girls laughed.

"Not funny," I said, standing. "I need coffee. What's good here?" I pointed at the various packets of coffee beans.

"Sit, I'll make you some coffee."

I sat while Natalie made us coffee and scrambled eggs. I wanted to help, but she shooed me away.

Penn and I sat in a comfortable silence while we watched Natalie work around the kitchen, preparing breakfast. The coffee was strong, but good.

My eyes flitted from Natalie to Penn.

"I knew you were different," Penn said mysteriously.

"Oh?" I said, arching my brows. "How so? I thought you were going to eat me the first time you saw me."

"Yeah, well," she started, a broad smile stretching her face. "You smelled delicious," — her eyes twinkled with humor, — "you still smell yummy, but no, I was testing you."

I shifted uncomfortably in my seat. It's not that I didn't want to be desired by women but eaten alive wouldn't do. I suspected Penn was sussing me out; here was I, a stranger with her sister, while she needed help. She needed to make sure I could protect them.

"And you understood your surroundings?" I asked Penn, swirling my right index finger in the air.

"Natalie kept me sane this past year." Penn stared at Natalie with nothing but love in her eyes. "She kept hope alive that one day I'd be freed. And when you entered the basement, I didn't like your smell at first; that leopard stink—"

"Snow leopard." I corrected.

"Whatever." She drawled, rolling her eyes. "What convinced me was the expression on your face that I recognized on my sister's face when Ian was being a dick to her. I knew you didn't like him either."

She was quiet for a moment then added, "Don't think I didn't notice how you stared at my sister." Her intense stare unnerved me.

I kicked her under the table and shook my head. There was too much going on at the moment and it wasn't the best time to talk about my feelings for a Komodo dragon shifter.

Natalie placed a plate full of eggs in front of me and rested a hand on my shoulder while she set a plate in front of Penn. When she didn't remove her hand, I glanced up and thanked her for the food.

"Do you like me?" she asked. Her face emotionless.

A fire seared throughout my body thinking about our moment outside. "You know I do." I thumbed behind me at the hole in the kitchen wall and garden beyond. "And you like me too. I felt it in your kiss."

I hated the power display leaning more toward her with me seated, so I stood up and stared down at her. My beast pushed to the front and a low growl escaped my lips. She seemed to visibly shrink within herself.

"Ooh, I felt that," Penn said, standing up. "I think that's my cue to leave." She hurriedly picked up her plate and left.

Natalie didn't move, she didn't even look away. I stepped forward, pressing my body against hers, and continued walking, pushing her backward.

I pressed her up against the far wall and reached for her hands, lifting them above her head, and pushing them against the wall. I squeezed her wrists but she didn't moan in pain or push me away. She tilted her head upward and parted her lips, welcoming me.

I leaned forward, ensuring she felt my hard body against hers, and licked her lips. "What do you want to do, Natalie?"

Her grin left me excited.

Chapter Fifteen

"I would never have thought you enjoyed this sort of thing. But now that I think about it, the signs were there," I whispered near the shell of Natalie's ear. I watched all the little hairs near her neck rise. With my index finger, I softly caressed down her spine and watched the goosebumps spread across her body.

My finger was still on her body as I walked around the dining table. Coming in behind her, I palmed her ass with both hands and rubbed down the outside of her thighs, squeezing when I reached near her knee and moved back up to her ass, this time on the inside of her thighs. Before I reached her delicate folds, I slapped each ass cheek hard, eliciting pleasurable moans from her.

I gently massaged her inner thighs, careful not to touch that delicate little flower that ached for my touch, for release.

Natalie continued moaning frustratingly, but she had to wait. I was playing. When she moaned again, I slapped each ass cheek again, harder, leaving pink palm prints.

Lee

When she realized I wasn't going to give her what she wanted, she relaxed on the table, waiting patiently while I continued massaging her ass and near her delicate pleasure spot that glistened in the light.

Beautifully displayed on the table, I had full view of Natalie's body, and I appreciated her vulnerability. For someone who was physically and mentally strong, she was still a woman who needed a tender caress, a delicate kiss against her cheek, along with a whisper letting her know she's stunning, wanted, and desired.

Beast growled inside my head, desperately wanting to make her ours now and forever. But it wasn't time, not yet. I needed to go slowly with Natalie, or she'd bolt faster than a horse out of the gates.

I couldn't contain myself, but I'd remain in control; for a short while. I brushed my hand against her slick slit and her warmth made me want more of her.

I stood back, leaving her needy, and admired the display; Natalie bent over the table, her legs spread, and her hands gripping the other side of the table. I didn't need restraints keeping her there, just a whispered command and she'd remain there, waiting patiently.

"You're a marvelous specimen, Natalie," I said in a seductive tone.

She shivered.

I approached her and stopped near her head. I reached for her arms and massaged her shoulders. Slowly, I bent near her head and said, "Are you ready for me, Nats?"

"Yes, Lee," she swallowed hard.

"Good," I growled near her other ear. "Because I've been waiting to feel you, touch you, and taste you since the moment you stole my chair." I kissed her neck near her ear and worked my way down her right shoulder while my hands roamed her back.

I walked around the table and massaged her wet pussy. She moaned, threatening to close her legs. I stepped between her legs, ensuring she didn't move her feet.

When she relaxed, I inserted a finger, pumping slowly inside of her. When I inserted two fingers, I continued my delicious assault on her body; maintaining my rhythm. She whimpered, clenching around my fingers. I continued pumping my fingers until her waves of pleasure dissipated.

"Stand up," I said, helping her move, and turned her around. I wanted to look into her pretty blue eyes and watch her expression. I moved strands of hair off her face, and her eyes were barely open as she licked her dry lips.

"How are you feeling?" I whispered.

"Umm, good," she said, smiling. She opened her eyes but was still unseeing.

I pulled her into an embrace, and she clung to me.

"Let's go to your room," I said. "You need some comfort after all that."

Natalie nodded into my chest.

I picked her up, carried her to the bedroom, and set her down gently on the bed and removed the robe.

I nudged her legs apart. "Natalie?" I waited her to look at me. She needed to be ready for me, and I needed her permission.

Natalie focused on me, her smile widening. She sat up, scooted to the edge of the bed, and reached for me. I stepped closer. She grabbed my hard cock, licked from the base to the tip, and cleaned the pre-cum.

I could die right now. Her warm mouth and tongue were heavenly as she sucked, licked, and massaged. If she continued doing that, I would finish.

Lee

"Wait," I blurted, and carefully backed away from her delectable mouth. "I don't want to finish now."

Natalie grinned mischievously and got onto her hands and knees and teasingly crawled to the top of the bed; her ass on display. Then she sat down, spreading her legs.

"Oh gods, you're going to kill me, woman." I climbed onto the bed and stalked my prey; to pleasure the woman my beast and I wanted.

Natalie scooted down, getting comfortable, and wrapped her legs around my body. She pulled me in for an embrace, her soft lips on mine, and kissed me. It was the most delicate kiss I'd ever experienced; filled with compassion, emotion, and soul.

I got lost in her. The world was far removed from where our bodies entwined, our hearts beat against the other, and our souls joined in the metaphysical realm. The movement between us brought us closer.

Natalie reached for my steel member and stroked gently. I grunted when she directed my cock at her wet entrance, nudging me in and I thrusted all the way.

Slowly, I exited, and just before leaving her completely; I thrusted harder. Natalie enjoyed the hardness and sharpness of my thrusts and I continued doing that until I was ready to explode. I stopped, waited a few seconds before continuing.

Natalie met my strokes with her own, and the sound of our lovemaking echoed within the house. I was sure Penn heard us, but we didn't care.

The moment heat spread within my body; I was close. Watching Natalie, and she, too, was on the edge. I quickened my movements and when our orgasms crashed into us; I slowed down, savoring the delicious feeling.

I wanted to collapse on top of her, instead I lay beside her, pulling her into the curve of my body.

She settled into a comfortable position, pulling my arm under hers and held my hand.

We fell asleep like that, and it was the most peaceful slumber I'd ever experienced.

Chapter Sixteen

I paced in Léon's office, fidgeting with my shirt. I wore Ian's clothing when we left his house but the moment I arrived at Léon's Labyrinth I changed into my clothing and burned Ian's.

Natalie sat on the two-seater couch, watching me intently. "You're going to walk a hole into the floor, Lee. Come," she said, patting the seat beside her. "Come, hold my hand." She wiggled her fingers.

I stopped pacing and glared at her. After the things we did together, sitting beside her would be the end of my meeting with Léon and the beginning of carnal pleasures for us.

"I promise not to touch you in places I know you'll love." She patted the seat again.

I couldn't resist her any longer and sat beside her, pulled her into my arms and kissed her passionately. When I let go, her mouth remained opened, and her eyes closed. She licked her lips and slowly opened her eyes.

"Hmm," she hummed satisfactorily. "That's all I'm going to say," she added with a grin.

Léon entered his office without glancing in our direction. I'd worked with him for many years and could never read his expressions and today was no different.

He threw a stack of files onto his desk and sat down. He pushed his chair in, leaning his elbows on the desk, and steepled his fingers. He narrowed his eyes.

Natalie flinched beside me.

I leaned into the chairback and pulled Natalie closer.

"Right, I've notified the council," he said gravely. "They have reviewed the footage of Ian attacking Lee, and the evidence regarding your sister's curse. And although they don't want your head on a stick, I must punish you," he said to Natalie. Then he turned his dark gaze on me. "Sebastian will see to your punishment, Lee. I'm disappointed in your behavior—"

"Léon, please don't punish Lee," Natalie interjected. "It was my fault. I kept him in the dark and then I didn't give him a chance to stop me from destroying Ian. And as you know, when I turn into my Komodo dragon, nobody can stop me. Not even a vampire." She arched an eyebrow.

Léon nodded, considering this. "I agree, Natalie. But I can't have my employees do things against my wishes and not suffer the consequences. Sebastian will see to it the punishment is fair."

When he stood, Natalie jumped to her feet.

"Come with me," he said and headed toward the door.

Natalie did as instructed and followed Léon.

"Go to the Leap, Lee. Sebastian is waiting for you there," Léon said before they exited.

Shit! I thought, standing slowly. The emptiness of the room left me uncomfortable and I didn't want to stay too long. I opened the door, hoping to at least say goodbye to Natalie, but they'd already disappeared down the hallway.

I wondered where Léon had taken her and what kind of punishment he'd be giving her. As much as I wanted to know more I had to brace myself for Sebastian's punishment.

Chapter Seventeen

I arrived at the Leap, and everybody was there. I received no notification that we had a meeting, and I couldn't help but wonder whether everyone was here to witness my demise. To be punished publicly. It would be an embarrassing event, but I'd hold my head high and take it like a man.

I groaned silently as I traversed through the house and out the back door toward the yard and forest beyond.

On any other night, I'd enjoy the fresh air and the smell of pine, then later the chase as we hunted under the full moon. Instead, I was miserable. I wondered what Léon did to Natalie and hoped I'd see her again or if he'd send her back to Krystal Creek on her own. His serious tone and stern warning left me on edge. I hoped she was all right.

The thought of Sebastian punishing me in front of everyone didn't sit well. I was a private person. I was naughty, but some things I preferred to keep for myself.

Someone lit the huge bonfire that stood in the middle of

the yard; the flames flared angrily to life, bathing everyone's faces in warm light.

In a circle around the bonfire they had placed chairs and tables with eats atop along with various alcoholic beverages.

It felt as though someone had smacked me with a stupid stick. What was going on?

Someone grabbed my shoulder. I ducked, spun around and almost planted my claw into their chest. When I realized it was Sebastian, I stopped myself from killing our leader, but I wouldn't really kill him. He was quicker than everyone.

"Are you okay?" Sebastian asked, chuckling.

"What's going on?" I asked, following him. "Where will you punish me?"

"Punish you?" he yelled. "No, Lee," — he shook his head, — "there will be no punishment. This is a celebration."

I stopped in my tracks and grabbed his arm. "Please explain, because right now I'm so confused. Léon said—"

Sebastian laughed. "Relax, Lee, come."

My beast growled; we were both annoyed.

I sighed frustratingly and followed Sebastian to the edge where our land joined our part of the forest. I smiled at the older were-leopards teaching the young cubs how to hunt; which they did from a place of compassion and safety.

We taught the young were-leopards the essentials of being a leopard and the rest came naturally. Unfortunately, those attacked and turned had to learn the basics quickly. Not all survived, and there were some who went completely off track, thinking it was fine to hurt others as they were hurt.

When I saw the back of Sebastian, I stopped before I

crashed into him. I needed to focus but my mind was on Natalie's safety.

When I focused on my surroundings once more, I couldn't believe my eyes. The vision before me was one of the most beautiful sights I'd seen in a long time, like something out of a fairy tale.

Surrounded by lush green trees, highlighted by the silver tendrils of moon dust, stood the most beautiful woman I'd ever seen. She wore a light-green silk dress that revealed her curves in all the right places. Her hair was up in a messy bun with flowers decorating it. And she stood barefoot, wearing the broadest smile I'd ever seen.

"Happy birthday, Lee," Natalie whispered. Her eyes sparkled with excitement.

"What?" I glanced stupidly in Sebastian's direction, but he'd already left and there was nobody else around.

It was only us and the quiet of the forest. It felt like some cheesy scene from a romantic comedy.

"Is this some kind of joke?" I asked nervously. "Will I fall into a pit filled with crocodiles?" I glanced at the ground, but all I saw was grass, twigs, and insects.

"Is this your punishment?" I asked, glancing up at her. "Did they tell you to tease me until I finally died?"

"You're an idiot," Natalie said. She didn't wait for my response. She closed the gap, but instead of stopping, she hiked up her dress and jumped into my arms.

I wrapped my arms around her, lifting her a bit more so she didn't hurt herself on my belt buckle, and smacked her ass cheek. "That's for tricking me." I smacked the other ass cheek. "And that's for stealing my chair in the bar."

Her smile lit my soul on fire. The sparkle in her eyes warmed my chest. She leaned closer, her mouth near mine, and smiled. "I like you, Lee. I don't want to have your baby now, but I'd like to spend a lot more time with you."

My heart raced at the possibilities, and I couldn't wait. I crushed my lips against hers, needing her closer. Her body heat seared my skin, and I wanted to rip the thin material from her body.

"Ah-hum," someone cleared their throat. Their presence was like a bucket of ice-cold water down my front.

I turned around and peered over Natalie's shoulder. "Asshole," I said, settling Nats carefully on the ground and holding her hand. "What are you doing here?"

"You know I would never miss my friend's birthday." Kai pulled me and Natalie into an embrace. "I'm relieved you're okay," he said, patting my shoulder. "When Sebastian told me what Ian did and how relieved everybody was that she had destroyed him," — he glanced at Natalie, — "I worried about your safety." He let us go and stood back. "We didn't know if Ian had fledglings under him, but luckily he didn't." His eyes flitted to Nats and smiled. "Welcome to the family."

"Thanks, Kai."

I looked between the two and growled. "You know each other?"

"Of course. How else were we going to get her here to surprise you?"

"And you cut your camping trip short just for me? Ah, buddy, you shouldn't have." I licked my lips, pretending to kiss Kai when he pushed me away.

"No, we're not that close, buddy." He punched my arm. "Natalie, keep your man in line," he chuckled.

"Your man?" I drawled. "Am I your man, Nats? Hmm. Am I?" I wiggled my eyebrows, pulling her closer and kissing chastely.

"Yes, you are, and I'm your woman."

"Enough of this icky stuff," Kai said, chuckling. "You can get freaky later. First, let's celebrate your birthday and Ian's demise." Kai turned and headed in the bonfire's direction and where more of the leopards had gathered.

"It looks like everyone is here," I said, jerking my chin in Penn's direction. "They even got your sister here." I squeezed Natalie's hand, and she leaned against my arm.

Considering how the day started, I was elated that it would end this way.

Chapter Eighteen

Dwayne combed his dirty fingers through his greasy hair as he watched Natalie and Penn laugh. He loved the way the flames cast their beautiful features in shades of red and yellow, reminding him of a painting he had on his wall.

Dwayne pulled his ruffled shirt down, tucked it into his pants and pulled it out again. The shirt was uncomfortable, and he silently cursed his servant for not ironing his clothing the way he specified. He would have another talk with her when he got home.

Twigs snapped behind him and he flinched. He moved deeper into the shadows of the forest, pushing leaves to one side and smiled. Penn had her back to him as she picked food off the plate.

Dwayne adjusted his crotch, thinking about Penn and Natalie in his company like before, remembering a time when all they had was each other. It was a dark time for them, but he escaped, too, and he had forgiven them for leaving him to die.

Voices traveled closer to his hiding spot and Dwayne

stopped breathing. His nictitating eyelid moved when he blinked. His forked tongue tasted the air; leopards. He resisted the urge to hiss and give away his location.

No. He needed to wait. Wait until the girls were alone before doing what he wanted. And this time, nobody would escape.

Next in the Shifter Days, Vampire Nights, & Demons in between Series

www.vinci-books.com/flynn

Where Secrets Hide in Shadow.

I knew searching for Penn's dark past was dangerous, but I followed her into those cursed woods anyway. Now we're trapped in a strange village where shadows move on their own and ancient secrets surface. As my attraction to her grows, I must choose: expose the truth about her family or lose her forever.

Turn the page for a free preview…

Flynn: Chapter One

Dwayne combed his dirty fingers through his greasy hair as he watched Natalie and Penn laugh. He loved the way the flames cast their beautiful features in shades of red and yellow, reminding him of a painting he had on his wall.

Dwayne pulled his ruffled shirt down, tucked it into his pants and pulled it out again. The shirt was uncomfortable, and he silently cursed his servant for not ironing his clothing the way he specified. He would have another talk with her when he got home.

Twigs snapped behind him and he flinched. He moved deeper into the shadows of the forest, pushing leaves to one side and smiled. Penn had her back to him as she picked food off the plate.

Dwayne adjusted his crotch, thinking about Penn and Natalie in his company like before, remembering a time when all they had was each other. It was a dark time for them, but he escaped, too, and he had forgiven them for leaving him to die.

Voices traveled closer to his hiding spot and Dwayne

stopped breathing. His nictitating eyelid moved when he blinked. His forked tongue tasted the air; leopards. He resisted the urge to hiss and give away his location.

No. He needed to wait. Wait until the girls were alone before doing what he wanted. And this time, nobody would escape.

Flynn: Chapter Two

I wiped my face with my right hand and scratched my beard, but my fingers got caught in the caked blood; I needed to shower.

Glancing at the fading bruises, it relieved me the cuts were healing, leaving behind dried blood on my now smooth skin.

I glanced at my swollen eyes as visions of the carnage flashed before me; blood, torn flesh, and body parts. Then distant memories echoed with moans from those hurt, followed by screaming and shrieking.

The events that had just taken place would haunt me forever.

I glanced up when Jude entered the bathroom, giving me the same expression I gave him; a *'what the fuck did we just go through?'* look.

I couldn't recall the fight with Shannon all those years ago being this gruesome, but it was Shannon's offspring who had caused the fight today; which was just as bad, if not worse.

Lee

Shannon reminded me of a mad scientist; he mixed various DNA of a human and a shifter animal to create supernatural hybrids. They started off as his children, until he locked them up in cages like animals, because he wanted supernatural soldiers who were his killing machines instead.

I shook my head, grateful Shannon was no more, but the son he created had followed in his footsteps. Like evil father, like evil son; I shuddered at the thought.

"How are you holding up?" Jude asked, his tone gentle, throwing his towel over his naked shoulder.

"I'll get through it," I said and tried to smile, but I wasn't fooling him. "How's Lee?" I asked, changing the subject.

"He's with Sebastian at the Leap. The leopards who followed Dwayne to his location have returned and they're busy devising a plan to get the sisters back safely."

Dwayne had kidnapped Natalie and Penn, his sisters, right from under our noses. Even with all the were-leopards there, and us, we couldn't defend the sisters against him. But he wasn't alone. Dwayne had an army of hybrid Komodo dragons on his side, and he could command them to do as he pleased.

We didn't have a chance to shift into our stronger beasts. When the first were-leopard went down, shriveled into a husk and died, I realized we didn't have a fighting chance; their venomous bites killed us quickly.

One thing everyone agreed to was that we couldn't leave the sisters with the madman. It wasn't in my DNA not to help, but the thought of going through another battle left me on edge. I'd experienced enough death and destruction to last me ten life times. Yet, I had to help Lee get Natalie and Penn back, even if it cost me.

When I didn't respond, Jude added, "All the shifters are

banding together." His tone was gentler. "They say Dwayne took the girls to the lab where Shannon had created them and his army. We're leaving tonight," he said with hard lines etched into his face.

Jude and I had been through a lot together, and this was one fight I didn't want him to go on without me.

We moved to Sterling Meadow round about the same time. He had no tiger clan to join, so he joined me and the lions with Troy's permission.

Then we started working for Léon, the Master Vampire of Sterling Meadow, in his warehouse and had been friends since. Plus, we're always with Kai and Lee, so their leopards always included us in their meetings and parties.

It wasn't just the shifters protecting the town, but the vampires under Léon's rule, too. Everybody joined forces to keep everyone safe from danger. Léon was one of the nicest vampires to work for, and one of the best supernaturals who wouldn't hesitate to help. He did whatever it took to ensure we were all out of harm's way.

And because of my work relationship with Léon, I now had a brother in Jude, Lee, and Kai. The four of us worked together, lived together, and protected each other. That was the main reason why I couldn't let Lee down. I had to help him get Natalie back; even if it cost me my sanity.

"You don't have to do this—"

"No, I'll go. We all do," I said, turning around. "Everyone would help me if I was in Lee's shoes."

"Yes," Jude said, shrugging. "But he didn't wake up in a pool of his mother's blood. You did. Everyone knows you have triggers."

I shook my head, expelling the memory of the slaughter I had found myself in when I was ten years old. My village had been destroyed, and all my people were butchered. My head was almost split in two, yet I survived with my mother's corpse on top of me, protecting me from blows meant for me.

"I have to help."

Jude grabbed my shoulder and squeezed. "You can join me in the back. We'll be protecting the first wave." He smiled sadly. "Then, once they're through, we'll hold back for any Komodo dragons trying to escape. We're better prepared this time." He smiled sinisterly, and it brought a smile to my face. When Jude behaved like this, he had something up his sleeve; and whatever *it* was, I knew it would kill the dragons before they reached us.

"You should shower, too." Jude hung his towel up and stepped into the open shower. "Get that muck off your skin."

Grab your copy…
www.vinci-books.com/flynn

About the Author

A Multi-genre author writing twisted endings...

N Gray is a USA Today Bestselling Author who lives in Cape Town, South Africa, with her daughter and adopted cat named Miss Beans.

During the day, she's an analyst and provider profiler for a medical insurance company. At night, she types on her curved keyboard, creating fictional characters some may love and others you want to kill yourself.

She writes in four genres: urban fantasy, thriller, horror, and paranormal romance.

She now writes under Natalie Michaels for her new thrillers and SD Syns for her new horrors.

Acknowledgments

Thank you to my readers, old and new, for taking a chance on my books.

You are the reason I write the stories I do. As long as you keep reading, I'll keep writing.

I'm truly humbled by your support and encouragement.

I write in as many genres as I love reading in. There are so many stories swarming inside my head that I could never just choose one.

Horror is my guilty pleasure. I love writing short stories filled with dark humour and the occult, with a twist ending.

Urban fantasy and paranormal romance are where I love to spend my time, and I have so many books planned that I don't have enough time *(but I'll get there)*.

And lastly, my thrillers. Who doesn't love sitting on the edge of their seat while reading about what goes on inside the antagonist's mind? Well, I love writing about them.